1-2 PUNCH!

LIGHTS OUT

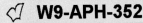

THE SUN HAD SET LONG BEFORE THE RUST BUCKET PULLED INTO THE SPRAWLING PARKING LOT.

The clock on the *Rust Bucket* dashboard showed it was Ben and Gwen's bedtime. But Ben and Gwen weren't getting ready for sleep. Instead, they stared out the window, their eyes blinking from the *bright lights* around them.

Nighttime was the best time for *Neon Land*.

The sign for the park rose high above them, five thousand blaring bulbs filling the darkness with brilliant light. Large spotlights waved back and forth through the sky.

Grandpa Max, sitting in the driver's seat of the Rust Bucket, had to squint. "*Wow.* This is even *brighter* than I imagined."

"*Neon Land* uses more electricity in one night than

BEN 10

1-2 PUNCH!

BY WRIGLEY STUART

ILLUSTRATED BY PATRICK SPAZIANTE

STINKFLY & CANNONBOLT

CARTOON NETWORK BOOKS

An Imprint of Penguin Random House

CARTOON NETWORK BOOKS
Penguin Young Readers Group
An Imprint of Penguin Random House LLC

TM and © Cartoon Network. (s18). All rights reserved. Published in 2018
by Cartoon Network Books, an imprint of Penguin Random House LLC,
345 Hudson Street, New York, New York 10014. Manufactured in China.

ISBN 9781524788551   10 9 8 7 6 5 4 3 2 1

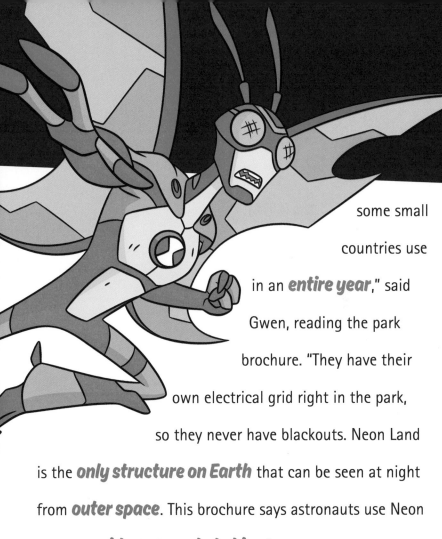

some small

countries use

in an ***entire year***," said

Gwen, reading the park

brochure. "They have their

own electrical grid right in the park,

so they never have blackouts. Neon Land

is the ***only structure on Earth*** that can be seen at night

from ***outer space***. This brochure says astronauts use Neon

Land to ***guide*** their ***rocket ships***."

"I bet aliens do, too," said Ben, his finger dangling over

the Omnitrix clamped on his wrist. With the press of a

finger, Ben's ***Omnitrix*** could turn him into any of ***ten alien***

creatures.

"Keep your hands off that, Ben," said Grandpa Max.

"We're here to **have fun**, not fight bad guys."

"As long as the **bad guys** know that," said Ben.

Grandpa Max laughed. "Sounds like a deal, Ben. No villains, no aliens. Agreed?" Ben nodded. "You guys ready?" Grandpa Max said.

"You bet," said Ben, jumping up from his cot. He yawned.

Grandpa Max arched his eyebrows. "Are you sure, Ben? I saw that yawn. It's pretty late, you know."

"That wasn't a yawn, it was just a, um, mouth stretch," said Ben. Gwen rolled her eyes. "Besides, I doubt I could sleep with all that **light pouring in** through our windows."

 "Then let's go, kids!" shouted Grandpa Max,

opening the Rust Bucket doors. Ben sprinted out of the vehicle, slowing down only to let his grandfather and Gwen catch up to him. They all **squinted** from the bright lights as they walked across the parking lot.

Grandpa Max bought **three tickets** from the ticket booth. He then handed Ben and Gwen dark **sunglasses**. He put a pair over his own eyes, too. "They gave me these. The lights here are so bright, you'll hurt your eyes if you don't wear them."

"Wearing sunglasses at night? Awesome!" said Ben. He put on his shades and then struck a pose. "Do I look cool?"

"No, you still look like a **dork**, as always," said Gwen with a laugh. When Ben shot her a dirty look, Gwen smiled. "You're a dork, but a **cool dork**." Ben continued frowning, but Gwen ignored her cousin's icy stare. "What ride should we go on first?"

They stood at the **front of the park**, in a large open space surrounded by twinkling thrill rides, gleaming snack huts, shimmering souvenir shops, and glittering game stands. Ben was thankful he wore sunglasses. "Let's go on that ride!"

Ben pointed to a long, tall coaster. Its tracks climbed up and up and up before sloping nearly straight down and then rising up into three consecutive loops.

The coaster's metal support beams glowed **red**, the cars on the track glowed **orange**, and giant **purple** strobe lights blinked on and off, on and off. Just staring at it hurt Ben's head, even with sunglasses. The glowing sign next to the ride read:

THE LUMINOUS LIGHT COASTER

Ben and Gwen took a step toward the ride when a loud **CRRAACK** filled the park. All the lights on the Luminous Light Coaster shut off.

The coaster wasn't the only thing *plunged into darkness*. The lights turned off at a small hot-dog stand and then at a small carousel.

"I thought you said this place couldn't have blackouts," said Ben.

"That's what the brochure said," explained Gwen, scratching her head.

Screams pierced through the now-dark air. One of the cars on the Luminous Light Coaster had stopped *upside down*, at the top of its largest loop. In the faint glow from other nearby lights, Ben could see a *hat* and *sunglasses fall*.

"Luckily they're *strapped into their seats*," said Grandpa Max. "Can you get them down, Ben?"

"I thought you didn't want me to turn into an alien unless a villain showed up?"

"Never mind that, Ben. Some rules are meant to be broken."

"I'll remember that the next time you tell me to stop eating potato chips in bed." Ben hit his palm against the **Omnitrix** and then, with a flash, he turned into the alien known as **Stinkfly**.

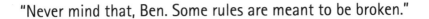

TIME IN!

The blue-and-orange winged alien was glad the remaining Neon Land lights didn't bother his fly-like alien eyes. He didn't think he could find sunglasses big enough to fit his **insect head**.

He soared into the air. Fortunately, Stinkfly **glowed in the dark**.

It helped him see where he was going as he flew higher and higher.

"**Hold on tight**, guys," Stinkfly said to the front seat passengers as he turned to face the others **still strapped in the car**. "I'll be back in a moment to help the rest of you down."

"Let me out now!" cried a large man in the back of the coaster. "I don't want to wait!"

"Oh stop creating a **stink**," said Stinkfly, who then laughed at his joke. "Get it? **Stink?** My name is *Stink*fly! **It's funny, right?**"

The man didn't laugh.

"I need better material," complained Stinkfly. He soared down, released the passengers on the ground, and flew back up to rescue more.

 A minute later, just as Stinkfly lowered the final

group of passengers, a **loud grumbling motor** sound began. The noise grew louder and louder, closer and closer. The ground **vibrated**.

"**Look!**" shouted Grandpa Max.

"What is that?" cried Gwen.

A **gigantic tractor** barreled through the front gates. The vehicle was as big as three, no, **four** regular-size tractors. It pulled a large cargo carrier, with a red-and-silver machine on top of it. The machine had a tub base as tall as a person and twice as wide, and a long rubber hose. It reminded Ben of an **oversize vacuum cleaner**.

The machine vibrated and rocked in place as lightning-bolt-shaped sparks flew into the hose. The air around it crackled. A **large man** stood next to the machine.

Stinkfly's mouth dropped open. The man next to the machine was Steam Smythe! The powerful and past-loving villain's bright red beard and mustache were impossible to miss.

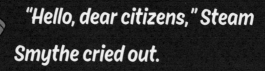

"Hello, dear citizens," Steam Smythe cried out.

"I am here to put an **end** to this ridiculous Neon Land. All this electricity! All this **waste**! Soon my **Power Defibrillating Vacuum** will suck up all the energy from this park. But this is only my first stop. I will then plunge the entire world into darkness.

Imagine! A world without electricity! No namby-pamby cell phones! No fancy-pancy televisions! No accursed video games!"

Stinkfly gulped. His eyes watered and his lips quivered. **"No video games?** A world without video games isn't a world I want to live in."

14

"You have to stop him, Ben," said Gwen, pointing at Steam Smythe.

"No problem for me." Stinkfly jumped up. He soared toward the villain, a fist held out.

Steam Smythe merely laughed. "You think you can stop me, you round-headed insect? My **Power Defibrillating Vacuum** doesn't merely suck electricity. It shoots it!"

The villain grabbed a **lever** on the base of the machine that was pointed to the word **IN**. He lifted it with a rusty **CREAK** so it was pointed to the word **OUT**. Steam Smythe pointed the hose at Stinkfly. "This Power Defibrillating Vacuum is now a Power Fibrillating Blaster!" Sizzling lightning darts shot out of the end of the hose and straight toward Stinkfly.

KZZT! KZZT!

The **powerful projectiles** whizzed through the air. A bolt shot over Stinkfly's head. The lightning darts flew to the right and left of him.

"You're a **terrible** shot," laughed Stinkfly, zigzagging up and down. "I can dodge those bolts all day long."

"Then it's a good thing it's nighttime!"

ZZZING!

A dart grazed Stinkfly's wing. Stinkfly sizzled from electricity, vibrating and shaking. He glowed bright orange. Then he **fell from the sky** like a lead balloon.

CRRAASH!

Stinkfly lay on the **hard concrete ground**, a soft moan sputtering from his lips. Gwen ran up to her cousin.

"Ben? Ben? **Are you okay?**"

"I want my **mommy**," mumbled a dazed Stinkfly, his eyes spinning.

TIME OUT!

Still dazed, Stinkfly transformed back into **Ben**.

"Well, **that stinks**," he groaned.

Meanwhile, Steam Smythe had moved the vacuum's lever back down and was sucking power from the park once again. As the **Power Defibrillating Vacuum** gobbled up electricity, more and more of the park plunged into darkness. Passengers were trapped on rides. Lights blinked off. Panicked, **frightened screams** filled the park.

Ben sat up, his arms and legs *aching* from his fall.

"Don't worry, Ben," said Gwen. "If you can't stop him, I will." She grabbed a rock from the ground and threw it at Steam Smythe. "Take that, you fiend!"

The rock bounced harmlessly at Steam Smythe's feet. The villain laughed. Gwen hurled another rock. This one bounced off the villain's head. "I admire your old-fashioned weaponry, lass. But you are *irritating* me," spat the villain. He aimed the nozzle of his weapon at Gwen and raised the *lever* of the machine.

Lightning darts flew from the hose once again. Stinkfly had been right: *Steam Smythe did have terrible aim.* But while the darts hit the ground near Gwen, one small spark bounced up and hit her leg. Gwen shook from the electricity filling her.

She gritted her teeth. "ZZZZZZ!" Her hair stood straight up and she glowed blue.

"Gwen! Look at me!" shouted Grandpa Max.

"ZZZZZZ…" grunted Gwen.

"Well, this is *shocking*," said Ben. "Get it? *Shocking?* "

Grandpa Max did not laugh.

"I really need to work on my jokes," complained Ben. "But no more funny business; *I'll stop Steam Smythe.*" Ben hit his Omnitrix, but nothing happened.

He hit it again, and again *nothing happened*.

"I guess it's still **powered down**. Which is sort of funny if you think about it, right? It's out of power, and Steam Smythe is sucking up power." Grandpa Max stared at Ben, blankly. "A little funny? No?" He sighed. **"Never mind."**

More electricity filled the oversize vacuum cleaner weapon. The machine seemed to grow a little bigger with every new bit of electricity. Lights around the park shut off, one after another.

Meanwhile, Gwen stopped vibrating, although her hair still stood straight up.

"Are you okay, Gwen?" asked Grandpa Max.

"Nice hairdo," giggled Ben.

"With all that electricity, I felt like I was going to **explode**." She scratched her head and stared at Steam Smythe and his **Power Defibrillating Vacuum**, which rocked and reeled, pulsated and vibrated, the metal bulging from the power inside it. "That machine looks pretty full, doesn't it? Maybe **too full** ?"

"What do you mean, Gwen?" asked Grandpa Max.

"I have an idea." Ben could almost imagine a **bright lightbulb** appearing over his cousin's head. "Ben, follow me!" Gwen sprinted across the park and Ben followed, while more and more of Neon Land *fell into darkness*.

"Where are we going?" asked Ben.

"I doubt that vacuum has a surge protector," said Gwen. She pointed to a small sign with an arrow that read:

POWER GENERATOR. THAT WAY.

"A surge what?" asked Ben, running as fast as he could to keep up with his **speedy cousin**. It was much easier

and faster to run or fly as an alien.

"A *surge protector*. That's what we plug computers into so they don't overload and short-circuit when they're plugged in. Did you see how much that defibrillating thingy was vibrating? If we can just overload that vacuum with too much electricity—"

"It might explode!" finished Ben.

"Exactly."

Ben and Gwen slowed down as they reached a small **grey metal generator** at the side of the park, partly hidden behind a cluster of bushes. It looked like a giant air-conditioning unit. Next to it was a sign with a small drawing of a lightning bolt and the words **WARNING! HIGH VOLTAGE!**

The door to its control panel was on the side. Gwen grabbed a black handle and swung the door open.

Ben and Gwen stared at a slew of wires and buttons. A single gauge read: **LOW / MEDIUM / HIGH / WAY TOO HIGH**. A needle fluctuated between **MEDIUM** and **HIGH**.

"Do you have your **sunglasses** on?" she asked Ben. Ben nodded. Gwen grabbed a small knob beneath the gauge and twisted it. The needle sprung to the right, past **HIGH** and all the way to the end, pointing to **WAY TOO HIGH**. The needle wiggled. The generator hummed loudly. Two wires sparked.

Most of the park's lights were **without power**, but not all of them. Those lights, the lights that still worked, **glowed brighter**. They wheezed and crackled and sizzled like bacon. A few lightbulbs **popped** from the intense power surging inside them.

"Let's see how that oversize vacuum cleaner likes eating all that," said Gwen.

Gwen and Ben ran back to the front of the park. When they reached Grandpa Max, they knew their plan was working. **The Power Defibrillating Vacuum grew bigger and brighter.** It shook faster and faster. Steam Smythe looked worried.

"No! It's taking **too much power**! What's happening?" cried Steam Smythe. He grabbed the lever that controlled the machine and began pushing it up, from **IN** to **OUT**. The lever broke off in his hand with a loud **SNAP**!

"No!" cried Steam Smythe. "What have I done?"

The machine bounced in place, higher and higher. Some metal screws burst off as the machine *bulged like a tire*. But there weren't many lights left in the park for the Power Defibrillating Vacuum to suck.

"We need *one more quick surge of power*," said Gwen, biting her lip.

ZZZAPP!

What seemed to be the final burst of light flew into the Power Defibrillating Vacuum nozzle. The machine rattled in place like some sort of crazy rocking chair. But despite its glowing and crackling, the machine did not explode.

"I've done it!" cried Steam Smythe in triumph.

Gwen shook her head. "So close, so close," she muttered. Then she looked at Ben. For a second, Ben was certain he had seen another lightbulb pop on over his cousin's head.

"Ben, quick! *Turn into Stinkfly again!* "

Ben didn't know why Gwen wanted him to become Stinkfly, but he knew better than to argue with her. She was right about things *far more often* than she was wrong.

BEN TAPPED HIS OMNITRIX AND—TIME IN!—HE WAS STINKFLY ONCE MORE.

The alien insect *glowed*. He was the only bright light in the park other than the brightly shining **Power Defibrillating Vacuum** next to Steam Smythe.

The red-bearded-and-mustached villain did not notice. He cackled with villainous pleasure. "Where should I go next? New York? Los Angeles? I will sap the energy from **every city**!"

"Now, Ben! Jump in front of the machine," shouted Gwen.

"But won't it suck all my power?" protested Stinkfly, admiring his own radiant glow.

"Exactly!"

Stinkfly soared toward the humming, rattling, and shaking machine. He flew right toward the nozzle in Steam Smythe's hands. **Stinkfly slowed.** He felt his power being drained. The nozzle in Steam Smythe's hands shook as electricity flew inside it. Stinkfly felt weak. He felt woozy. He **tingled** and **shook**. The light surrounding him dimmed. But the Power Defibrillating Vacuum was shaking even more than it had, its metal seams threatening to pop off.

"What are you doing, you scoundrel?" Steam Smythe cried to Stinkfly. "Get away! Shoo fly! Shoo!"

But it was too late. Stinkfly's power had been sucked dry and he landed on the ground. The Power Defibrillating Vacuum stopped glowing for a moment. It stopped vibrating. A strange calm came over the machine. Then suddenly . . .

KABOOM!!!

The vacuum exploded into a million pieces; small shards of vaporized and melted metal pelted the ground. A cloud of smoke rose into the air. When the cloud settled, the machine was gone and left in its place was a pile of metallic dust.

 Steam Smythe was covered in soot. **He sneezed.**

"**My machine!** My beautiful machine! What have you rascals done?" cried the bad guy.

TIME OUT! BEN TURNED BACK INTO HIMSELF.

Angry steam erupted from Steam Smythe's ears. He howled like a crazed wolf. "You may have stopped me now, but **I'll be back**!" he declared. The villain rose into the air, a **jetpack** strapped to his back shooting out small flames. The flames burned brightly in the still nearly pitch-black park.

"You haven't seen the last of me!" shouted the villain, now flying away. "The power to this park may be restored soon, but I will restore the power of the past. Mark my words, **you scallywags**!"

With his **Omnitrix** powered down, Ben could do nothing but watch the villain soar off.

In the dark, however, Steam Smythe couldn't see where he was going. Ben and Gwen could see the flames shooting out from his jetpack when they heard a loud **CRUNCH** and **BANG**.

"I think he just flew into the **Luminous Light Coaster**," said Gwen.

"I bet he's steamed," said Ben, nodding his head. "Get it? Steamed? As in Steam Smythe?" Gwen didn't say anything and Ben sighed. "Never mind."

Up above they heard another **BANG** and a painful "Ow! My head!" followed by another **CRUNCH** and an "Ow! My back!" Finally, the flames shooting from the jetpack's bottom grew more and more distant as Steam Smythe drifted far away.

"Good job, kids," said Grandpa Max, giving Gwen

and Ben a big hug. "**You saved the park.** But without power, this entire place is going to be shut off for a while. We should head back to the Rust Bucket for some shut-eye."

Soon, the three of them were walking out of the park, across the parking lot toward the **Rust Bucket**. As they walked, Ben yawned, and the yawn quickly spread to Gwen and then Grandpa Max.

"Sorry, guys," said Ben. "I know yawns are contagious."

"We're all tired," said Grandpa Max. "I'm looking forward to getting back to the Rust Bucket and catching some sleep."

Ben nodded. "As soon as we get back to the Rust Bucket, it's **lights out** for me." He laughed. "Get it? **Lights out?**" No one laughed. Ben shook his head. "I really need better jokes."

THE END

"WE'RE HERE, KIDS. SALEM TOWN!"

said Grandpa Max from the driver's seat of the

Rust Bucket.

"Do we have to go?" asked Ben, frowning.

Gwen threw her cousin a dirty look. "I think it will be *fun*."

"You think reading is fun," groaned Ben.

"It is." Gwen lifted the **big black book** she had been

holding on her lap. She looked at the title in bright yellow:

The History of Salem.

"If you tried reading sometime, you'd think reading was fun, too."

"I read **sometimes**," Ben insisted. "I read the cover of my

new **video game** just last week." When Gwen threw Ben

another dirty look, he added, "**It's summer.** You're not supposed

to read during the summer. **Everyone** knows that."

With a sigh, Gwen threw her book into a small brown satchel, threw the satchel over her shoulder, and followed Ben and her grandfather out of the Rust Bucket.

"You guys will *love* this place," said Grandpa Max as they walked into Salem Town. "I used to come here as a kid. *I loved it.*"

"Why do they call it Salem Town?" asked Ben.

"Because it's made to look just like a small American village from the *1600s*. A famous town from back then was *Salem, Massachusetts*."

"It looks like they haven't done anything to fix this place since the 1600s," said Ben.

He looked around at the **peeling paint** and **cracked windows** on the old wooden buildings. Dead bushes lined the sides of the houses and a big church. The dirt roads were filled with **divots**, and the gas lampposts on the side leaned crookedly. Even the sign in front that read **SALEM TOWN** was chipped and falling over.

Grandpa Max frowned. "I heard this place wasn't in very **great shape** anymore."

A **short, plump woman** walked toward them, next to a **tall man** with a big black beard. They reminded Ben of pilgrims. The woman wore a simple grey dress and white apron. The man wore a black coat, short pants with white stockings, and a tall hat with a large gold buckle.

"Good morrow," said the woman. "My name is Mary. **How do thee fare?** "

"We fare well, thank you, kind lady," said Gwen.

"This is going to be a long day," Ben muttered to himself.

The man took off his hat and bowed. "**Welcome, friends.** I am John, one of the town's elders and your humble servant. Pray forgive the appearance of our town." He frowned and slumped his shoulders. "I regret they are tearing down this park next week to build a new **shopping mall**."

"They can't do that!" exclaimed Grandpa Max.

"**...Fast enough,**" added Ben, watching a shingle fall off the roof of a building.

The bearded man sighed. "I trust you shall enjoy your visit today. Just be careful of falling shingles." He bowed again. Grandpa Max and Gwen bowed back. Ben rolled his eyes.

"I can't believe they are tearing this place down," said a frowning Grandpa Max.

"I can't believe they didn't tear this place down **years ago**," said Ben.

Gwen opened the book she held. "I agree with Grandpa Max. I think it's a **shame**. We can learn a lot from our past. I was reading all about the Salem Witch Trials in this book."

"Did you say witches?" asked Ben.

Salem Town suddenly got a lot more interesting.

"Not *real* witches," said Gwen. "Back more than *three hundred years ago* in Salem, a group of innocent people was accused of being witches and hanged."

"How do you know they were innocent?" asked Ben. "Maybe they were witches."

Gwen threw her cousin a big frown. "There are *no such things as witches*, Ben. Everyone knows that."

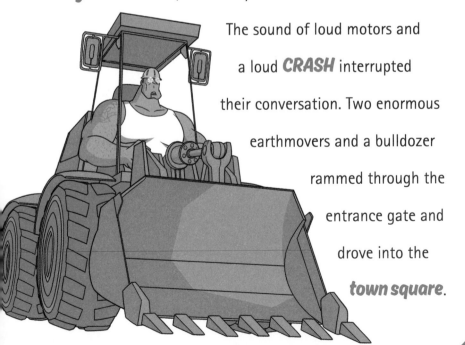

The sound of loud motors and a loud **CRASH** interrupted their conversation. Two enormous earthmovers and a bulldozer rammed through the entrance gate and drove into the *town square*.

"Stop! I pray!" cried John, holding his buckled hat as he ran toward the machines.

He waved his arms. "Halt, I say! *Halt!* You aren't supposed to be here until *next week*!"

The man driving one of the earthmovers stared forward. His *glazed eyes* spun around in circles. The crane of the earthmover he drove dug a mound of dirt and grass out of the lawn and then *dumped it on the side*. The other earthmover did the same. Its driver's eyes also spun round and round.

"The drivers look like they are in some sort of *trance*," said Gwen.

"Maybe a witch put a spell on them," said Ben.

Gwen spun her own eyes. "Stop it. *There is no such thing as magic, Ben.*"

"Stop!" cried John. "What are you doing?"

Meanwhile, the bulldozer rammed into a small shed,

knocking it over. The wooden walls crumbled into a heap. The eyes of the driver spun in wild circles, just like the eyes of the other men.

"What's going on?" asked Gwen.

"Stop! Stop!" shouted John, stomping up and down. But the drivers didn't pay attention to him. The earthmovers continued removing piles of dirt. The bulldozer demolished a small water fountain.

"It's like those earthmovers are digging for something," said Gwen.

A crane scooped a large chunk of earth, revealing a thin ***wooden box*** that had been buried deep in the ground. The earthmovers stopped their digging and stood still, their ***motors idling***. The drivers sat in their cabs as if waiting for something.

And that something was here. Above the ***town square***, the evil sorcerer Hex floated down from the sky.

"I thought you said there was no such thing as magic," Ben said to Gwen.

"I was sort of wrong about that," Gwen admitted.

The grey-skinned and ancient villain **landed softly** on the ground. He wore his familiar red-and-black hooded robes. His face was painted to resemble a **skull**. "Could it be mine at last?" he asked, his voice trembling with excitement.

Hex knelt down and lifted the **wooden box** from the ground. With shaking hands, he opened the box's lid and then removed a **large, thick book** from inside it. Strange **bright yellow symbols** were drawn on its ancient black leather cover. The magical villain's eyes glowed.

"Yes, **it's mine**!" Hex cried out. He held the book over his

head in triumph. "Behold: *The Book of Salem*!
The ancient witch rituals that have been lost for
nearly three hundred years are mine at last!"

Ben turned to Gwen and frowned. "That doesn't sound good, does it?"

"No, not really," agreed Gwen.

Hex's mouth twisted into a diabolical smile. "In this book
resides the *Ancient Salem Curse*, a curse that will turn
anyone in the world into a mindless zombie who will follow
my every command!"

"You need to do something, Ben," said
Grandpa Max.

"I'm on it." Ben twisted the *Omnitrix*
on his wrist and slapped his palm against it.

TIME IN!

WITH A FLASH, BEN GREW BIGGER, WIDER, AND STRONGER.

In an instant he was the powerful, yellow-armored, white-and-black alien known as **Cannonbolt**. He glared at Hex.

"You think you're taking over the world? I'm taking you ... out!"

Cannonbolt curled himself into the shape of a **giant ball**. He bounced twice and then spun toward Hex. As he rolled, he went **faster** and **faster**, ready to flatten the evil sorcerer.

Hex wasn't frightened. "My Bolts of Destruction will stop you!"

The villain **mumbled an incantation** and sparks sputtered from his hand. Lasers flashed and then flew from his fingertips toward Cannonbolt.

POW! BAM! CZZZT!

The laser beams smashed into Cannonbolt, but his armor plating was strong. Very strong. The lasers **bounced off** the rolling alien, zooming off in every direction. One laser flew and hit a tree, blowing it into a million pieces.

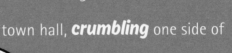

Another blast burst through the walls of the town hall, **crumbling** one side of the building. Another blast zipped through three lampposts. The lights crumbled into **tiny shards**.

Gwen and Grandpa Max ducked to avoid being hit by more deflected blasts.

Cannonbolt stopped rolling and looked around at the destruction. "Sorry about that. **My bad.**"

"We need to get that book," said Grandpa Max to Gwen.

"Leave it to me," said Gwen.

Hex threw **three more blasts** at Cannonbolt. The alien lifted his arm, blocking the beams with his armor and sending them straight back toward the villain. Hex dived out of the way. The beams hit a group of trees and **shattered** them into tiny toothpicks.

Meanwhile, Gwen **crept** toward the villain. During the

confusion, Hex had dropped the **Book of Salem**. If Gwen could grab it, she could stop the villain's evil plot.

Cannonbolt curled himself into a ball once more and rumbled toward Hex. The ground shook beneath his **powerful roll**.

Hex **dived** out of the way.

But those extra seconds were just what Gwen needed. She snatched the **Book of Salem** and dashed away, holding the book tightly in her hands.

Hex spotted Gwen running away.
When he spoke, his voice roared with anger.

"**Who dares** mess with Hex? **Who dares** steal my **book**!"

He pointed his hand toward Gwen. Flames danced from his fingertips.

"Um, Ben? **A little help!** " cried Gwen.

"I've got this," said Cannonbolt.

CANNONBOLT TURNED BACK INTO BEN.

Ben frowned. *"Never mind,"* he groaned.

Hex waved his fingertips.

"Foolish mortals," he cried. "I'll easily

dispose of the likes of you two."

He *aimed* his sizzling fingers at Gwen.

"Get away from us!" cried Gwen, hurling the only thing

she held at Hex: *the book*.

The black-covered book sailed into the air. Hex laughed.

"Silly girl! That's all I wanted."

Hex caught the book and mumbled a *series of magic*

words. In a moment, he had *disappeared* in a cloud of

thick smoke.

Grandpa Max ran over to Gwen and Ben. When he reached

them, he gave each of them a *big squeeze*.

"I'm so happy you kids are *okay*. That Hex guy gives me the *creeps*."

He patted Ben and Gwen on the head. "Gwen, I'm awfully glad you saved us, but why did you throw the book at him? I thought we needed to keep that book away from Hex's clutches, not give it to him."

Gwen removed a book from her brown satchel. "The *Book of Salem* is right here. I threw my *history book* at him, not this."

"That was *fast thinking*, Gwen," said Grandpa Max.

"But as soon as Hex realizes he has the wrong book, he'll be back."

Gwen and Ben *nodded*. They all knew the evil wizard wouldn't be gone for *very long*.

With Hex gone, John and Mary rushed out into the street, hollering with joy. *"Huzzah! Huzzah!"*

John clapped Ben, Gwen, and Grandpa Max on their

backs. "We are forever in your debt."

"It was nothing," said Gwen, blushing.

"He'll be back," Grandpa Max warned.

"Until then, may we show you our *gratitude*?" asked John.

"We should probably get ready for Hex," said Grandpa Max.

"But we're serving complimentary apple pie and chocolate cake in the dining hall to celebrate," said John.

"Did you say *chocolate cake*?" asked Ben, his eyes wide.

"And *apple pie*?" asked Gwen, licking her lips.

Grandpa Max wagged his finger at Gwen and Ben. "There are *more important things* than cake and pie."

"Sure. Such as *ice cream*," agreed Ben.

"We have *ice cream*, too," said John.

Grandpa Max sighed. "Maybe we have time for *a little dessert*." His stomach rumbled loudly. Ben jumped up and high-fived his cousin.

As they followed John to the dining hall, Ben looked over at the construction vehicles. The bulldozer and the earthmovers were still there, their motors purring, but the drivers stared out *mindlessly*, eyes spinning, waiting for Hex's next order.

Ben hoped that order would come much later— after pie, cake, and ice cream.

A few minutes later, the Tennysons all sat in the dining hall. The room looked almost like a room built *three hundred years ago*. The large wooden rafters of the ceiling were rotting, the wooden tables were cracked and chipped, and the wooden floor had dozens of large holes. Ben just hoped the place didn't collapse while they were still eating inside it.

A *half-dozen people* sat in the dining hall. They all wore clothes that reminded Ben of *pilgrims*.

"This food is *delicious*," said Grandpa Max between mouthfuls of cake.

"We follow the **same recipes** as those from hundreds of years ago," said John. "No preservatives or artificial flavoring."

"What do you think, guys?" Grandpa Max asked Ben and Gwen.

"MFLLTGPP," said Ben, his mouth too full to speak, but a big smile on his face.

"MFLLTGPP," Gwen agreed, her mouth also too full, and also smiling broadly.

"But we should eat quickly," Grandpa Max warned them. "We don't know when Hex—"

He never finished his words. He **dropped** his spoonful of ice cream as he stared at Hex, now **floating through the wall** of the dining hall. The sorcerer hovered in the air, glaring around the room. He held **Gwen's book** in his hand and flung it across the room. It crashed into the wall.

"Bah! **A history book!** " he wailed. "Where is that accursed girl? Where is the one who stole my book?"

When he spied Gwen, he pointed a long grey finger at her.

"You! You have the **Book of Salem**!"

He cupped his hands together and a **bright red cloud** rose up from his palms.

"Quick, Ben!" shouted Gwen. "Stop him!"

"No problem," said Ben. He lifted his hand to tap his **Omnitrix**. Hex would be no match for an alien! But before Ben could complete his hand slap, Hex mumbled a few words. The **cloud** hovering in Hex's hands blew across the room.

SWOOSH!

Ben felt frozen solid. His hand remained in the air hovering above the Omnitrix. No matter how hard he tried, his hand was stuck in the air.

He couldn't move.
No one could.

"A simple **freezing spell** will ensure

I get the **Book of Salem** without any more delay,"

chuckled Hex. The **Book of Salem** sat inside Gwen's brown

satchel on an empty seat next to her. The evil wizard floated

to their table and snatched the **Book of Salem** out from her

bag. He was so close to Ben, Ben could practically touch him.

But Ben couldn't do anything. He couldn't hit his **Omnitrix**.

He couldn't punch Hex. He couldn't scratch a horrible itch on his

elbow.

The sorcerer examined the **cover** of the book. He caressed

its leather. He smelled its ancient dust. He opened it and

scanned its pages.

**"Yes, this is it. This is the Book of Salem. There will
be no more trickery. The world will be mine to rule."**

Staring at the book, Hex *lost all interest* in Ben, Gwen,

and the others. He floated away from them *toward the*

wall and then rammed into it, headfirst, with a loud *BANG*!

Hex looked up, rubbed the tip of his nose, cursed, and

muttered a spell. Then he floated through the wall of the dining hall like a ghost.

As soon as Hex left the room, his *freezing spell wore off*. Grandpa Max looked at the spoon he had dropped on the table. Ben's hand completed its slap atop the *Omnitrix*.

TIME IN!

BEN WAS NOW CANNONBOLT ONCE AGAIN.

"He's going to *rule the world*," said Gwen.

"Not if I stop him first," said Cannonbolt. The alien *flexed his muscles* and rolled himself into a *large ball*. He barreled across the floor toward where Hex had floated.

"Ben, the door is *that way*!" cried Gwen, but it was too late. Cannonbolt *burst through the wall* of the dining hall, the wood splintering and the windows shattering.

Hex floated away, too interested in the **Book of Salem**

to pay attention to anything else. But as Cannonbolt rumbled closer and closer, the villain **turned around**. Hex had just enough time to react.

He swooped to his left as Cannonbolt careened past him. **Cannonbolt kept rolling**, bowling through the walls of a small barn.

"Sorry," said Cannonbolt.

Cannonbolt twisted around and **raced toward Hex** once more. The villain dashed to his right.

Cannonbolt rolled over a **fence**.

"Sorry."

Cannonbolt **changed directions** again. This time, Hex flew

up and out of the way. Cannonbolt rolled over a **statue**.

"Sorry," said Cannonbolt. He kept rolling and
rolling over things. "And sorry, and sorry ..."

Hex muttered a spell. Flames sparked from his fingertips.

As he had done before, flaming laser beams flew toward

Cannonbolt. "My **Bolts of Destruction** will destroy you!"

BING! BOUNCE! CRZZZZZNG!

Like before, the lasers **bounced off** Cannonbolt's nearly

indestructible armor. The beams flattened signs, ignited trees, and

blew holes through building walls.

CRASH! SMASH! BANG!

Cannonbolt stopped rolling and scanned all the damage

around him. **"Sorry** about all that, too."

Grandpa Max and Gwen watched from behind a large

tree. "Good thing they were planning on **demolishing**

this place in a few days anyway," said Grandpa Max.

"Looks like Ben's doing the job for them," said Gwen.

"Enough!" cried Hex, floating high into the air. He held the book

of spells in front of him. "I will now chant the magic spell that

will force everyone to **obey me**! You will all soon be **mindless**

zombies, helpless to do anything but follow my every word."

"Stop him, Ben!" yelled Gwen.

Cannonbolt rolled himself into a ball, but Hex was already

chanting the words. *"Incandesto imbecilo chowder-embrio!"*

The sky around Hex **rippled with energy**. Hex seemed to

grow larger. An energy field of bright violet surrounded him and

pumped in and out like a **heartbeat**.

Gwen could barely look. "I don't want to be a mindless

zombie," she sobbed.

"It could be worse," said Grandpa Max.

"How?"

"I'm not sure. Maybe it **couldn't** be worse."

ZZZOOOOMM!!

A **ripple of energy** shot out from Hex, a jet stream of pulsing light hurtling toward Gwen and Grandpa Max.

"Noooo!" cried Cannonbolt as he rolled toward Gwen and Grandpa Max. The ripple grew closer. Cannonbolt rolled faster.

Ripple. Roll. Ripple. Roll.

Gwen and Grandpa Max screamed.

The ripple and roll met at the same time. The energy field **bounced off** Cannonbolt's armor. It rebounded back, back, back. And **directly into Hex**.

KAPLOOZZZ!

Cannonbolt stopped rolling. Gwen and Grandpa Max stopped yelling.

All was silent as Hex's eyes spun in circles. The sorcerer's legs and arms shook. His body **slowly sank** to earth.

"What just happened?" asked

a very confused Cannonbolt.

"I think Hex just cast a spell for him to blindly follow . . . *himself*?" guessed Grandpa Max.

"I will *obey*," mumbled Hex. "I will *follow*." Still muttering softly, Hex drifted away, his eyes spinning and his mind a zombielike cloud.

TIME OUT! CANNONBOLT TURNED BACK INTO BEN.

He continued to watch Hex. "I think he'll be *talking to himself* for a while," Ben guessed.

"We should *destroy* that book," said Grandpa Max. Hex had dropped the *Book of Salem* when he floated away. Gwen reached down and picked it up. She tossed it *into a small fire* that blazed nearby, the only thing left of a small food stand that Cannonbolt had rolled over.

"Sorry about that," said Ben.

As soon as the book touched the flames, a large spark flew

high into the sky. *The book turned to charcoaled ash.*

John, the village elder, clasped Ben on the shoulder.

"*Huzzah!* You saved us again! We shall always be indebted to you, young sir. As long as Salem Town is around, you will *always be welcome* here."

Ben looked around. Most of the buildings were either *completely destroyed* or *heavily damaged.* The buildings that weren't destroyed were falling apart anyway. The men from the bulldozer and earthmovers walked over. Their eyes were no longer glazed. *Hex's spell had worn off.*

"Do you mind if we *finish destroying* this place?" asked the driver of one of the earthmovers. "Most of the work was done by that armor-plated alien guy and the scary fellow in the skeleton paint, anyway."

"It shouldn't take us very long," added one of the other men.

John frowned and nodded. *"Go ahead."* To Ben he said, "Well, you *would have been* welcome here, if there was a here anymore."

Minutes later, Ben, Gwen, and Grandpa Max walked out of the park that **used to be** Salem Town. Bulldozers and earthmovers razed the few buildings that were left.

Before they reached the Rust Bucket, Gwen gave her grandfather a **big kiss** on the cheek. "I'm sorry this place **wasn't as awesome** as you remembered, Grandpa."

"Thanks, Gwen," said Grandpa Max, giving her a big hug.

"But I've got a lot of new memories of this place I'll always cherish."

"Do you mean memories of me defeating Hex?" asked Ben.

"Actually, I was talking about memories of that **apple pie**," said Grandpa Max, patting his stomach. "That was really good."

"That's my favorite memory of this place, too," said Gwen, licking her lips.

Ben frowned and then shrugged. "Actually, I think my favorite memory is the **chocolate cake**," he admitted.

THE END